Kids' Stuff

Zoe heard a scuffling noise. She tried to open the door but it wouldn't budge. Something was blocking it.

She heard footsteps running down the corridor. And laughter.

The empty classroom was big and gloomy. And it was scary in here on her own.

How was she going to get out? How long would she have to stay in here? If she shouted, would anybody hear her over the music?

She slipped down onto the floor and curled up into a ball. *What am I going to do, Zara?* she whimpered.

Kids' Stuff

Sue Vyner

Illustrated by
Robin Lawrie

Evans Brothers Limited

Published by Evans Brothers Limited
2A Portman Mansions
Chiltern Street
London W1U 6NR

First published 2001

British Library Cataloguing in Publication Data
Vyner, Sue
Kids' Stuff
1. Children's Stories
I. Title
823.9'14 [J]

ISBN 0237523302

Series Editor: Julia Moffatt
Designer: Jane Hawkins
Printed in Malta by Gutenberg Press Limited

Chapter One

It wasn't that Zoe still believed in Zara. Imaginary friends were kids' stuff after all.

But she had been doing it since she was little. So she was used to discussing things with Zara.

It was just a habit.

One she couldn't break.

Like biting her nails...

When she was little everyone knew about Zara. Thought it was hilarious. Laughed out loud. And she hadn't minded.

But she'd mind now. Couldn't bear it if they laughed. Or worse – thought she was a nut case.

So Zara, soul mate, was now Zoe's secret.

It was such a relief chewing things over with her though. Like how much her older sister Mel got to her. Like how much her tearaway younger brother

Tod upset her. And like how much her careworn parents misunderstood her.

Zara eased the loneliness. Because Zoe was lonely. Strange that – in the middle of a family like hers.

The trouble was, she was different from the rest of them. Whereas her sister hated books and doing homework, Zoe was the opposite. And whereas her brother found it impossible to stay out of trouble, she found it easy. And her parents just didn't understand her.

If only I had my own room, Zara, she wrote in her diary as she sat cross-legged on her bed looking round the room she shared with Mel. *But at least it's better since Dad separated the bunk beds. One bed on each side of the room. One side of the room mine.*

She got off the bed and teetered along the red line painted across the middle of the room like a tight rope walker. Then went back to her diary. *Dad laughed when we painted this, but I think it was a brilliant idea.*

She surveyed her side of the room. A space for doing her homework and a space for her books. Soft toys arranged at the bottom of the neatly-made bed, others at the top. 'A place for everything and everything in its place,' Mum always said with

wonder. Because Mum couldn't keep anywhere tidy.

And nor could Mel. On Mel's side, clothes spilled out of a bulging cupboard onto the unmade bed and over the floor. Homework books lay on the floor, the pages rumpled and dirty. Make-up was scattered everywhere. Chewing gum stuck to everything that had a surface. *And it's not as if she's just going through a phase*, she wrote, working herself up into a temper. *Well, if it is a phase it's lasted fifteen years.*

She bit at her nails. Then made an effort to calm down and think of something nice.

At school this morning, Zara, Mr Peters told us to think about something nice, and then to picture it in our heads. Her eyes lit up as she wrote. *And straight away I remembered seeing this amazing bird, dipping its l-ong neck into next door's pond. It was a heron. Really fantastic. And it was stealing Mr Jones's precious fish. Mr Jones went mad!*

She giggled. Then looked thoughtful. *The rest of the class all thought about pop stars or footballers though. Drooling like. And I was the odd one out.* She chewed her pen. *So what's new?*

Her mind raced on as she wrote, *Then Mr Peters said: "Pleasure!" Like it was an announcement. "Proper word? – Hedonism," he said. And wrote the word on the board. "Do me the honour of remembering this word. That will indeed give me great pleasure." Mr Peters always talks like he's swallowed a dictionary, Zara.*

She paused, then wrote on, *Hedonism is a great word for Mel. All she ever thinks about is the "pursuit of pleasure".* Someone else popped into her head too. *And it fits Frankie James to perfection.*

At the thought of Frankie James, Zoe's mood plummeted. Because Frankie James just happened to be everything Zoe wasn't and thought she never would be. Which reminded her of the Christmas concert at school. The dreaded concert.

Ye-Olde-English-Country-Dance, she wrote. *That's what I'm doing in the concert. It seemed like a good idea at first, but now I think it's just boring. While Frankie James gets to do a modern dance routine that has everyone riveted to the spot.*

She pushed her short skinny legs angrily along the bed and inspected them, then wrote, *Frankie's got legs that go on for ever.* She fingered her short mousy brown hair. *And she dyes her hair a different colour to suit her every mood.* Next, she leapt off the bed and rushed to the mirror, puckered her mouth up and pouted. *She's got these pouty lips, Zara*, she said through puckered lips. *And her eyes. They're amazing. Every-Colour and No-Colour.* Zoe blinked furiously till her brown eyes moistened then fluttered them in the mirror. But it only made her look like she was about to burst into tears. She wiped them angrily with the back of her hand.

Zoe hated the way she looked. Nearly fourteen years old, and with almost the same body she'd had when she was ten. She went back to her diary.

Frankie must wear at least a size 36 bra! she wrote longingly. *And while I'm pathetically shy, she's got enough confidence to die for. She'll talk to anybody. Frankie's so gabby some teachers end up nearly throttling her.*

She flopped back on the bed, turned to the wall and buried her head in the crook of her arms. *The trouble is, nobody notices me, Zara,* she whispered. *Not at home. Not at school. I may as well be invisible.*

Chapter Two

It was the first performance of the school Christmas concert. To be performed in front of the rest of the school. Could *anything* be worse?

Zoe kicked the table leg.

The atmosphere in the classroom where they were changing was charged with excitement. But while everyone else was prancing around admiring themselves, Zoe was reluctant to even put her costume on. If you could call it a costume.

Skirt. Blue and white check. With frill.

Petticoat. White. With frill.

Blouse. White. With frill.

Pumps. Black. Ankle socks. White.

And it got worse. A ribbon in her hair. Red.

Other girls in the same gear looked like thirteen and fourteen year olds in costume. But *she* looked like an infant. While Frankie James? She, and the two others doing the routine with her, were dressed in tight red satin trousers that in Frankie's case matched her hair – at the moment – and revealed a pierced belly button. They wore gold handkerchief-tops. And had on the full-make-up-thing. Zoe had tried not to let on she was staring when Frankie put the make-up on. But there'd been plenty of time to watch. It'd taken her for ever.

She looks older than Mel, Zara. And Mel can pass for eighteen.

Frankie brushed past Zoe's table. 'What are you staring at?' she said.

Zoe cringed. 'I wasn't staring,' she mumbled.

'You could have fooled me,' Frankie said and swept past.

Zoe's eyes followed Frankie round. Frankie's dance was the finale of the show and everyone rated it.

Her lips quivered. Frankie's music only had to begin for a buzz of excitement to start. And today, with the lights and the audience *and* that costume, she was in her element. Blow the rest of the concert, she all but said as she strutted round the classroom.

The concert was called, 'Christmas through the Ages. A Celebration of Music and Dance'. And it was after an introductory musical extravaganza that the country dance got things going on the dance front. Building up to Frankie's dance which brought things bang up to date and to a cracking close.

Miss Winston, Deputy Head, appeared at the classroom door waving her arms.

'QUIET!' she bellowed.

They must have heard her in the hall. Where there'd be an instant hush. Miss Winston had that effect on everyone.

'Settle *down*,' she said, her voice dipping on the *down* and having the intended effect. 'The show's about to start.'

It was time for the dreaded country dance. And as Zoe waited in the wings for it to start, her body was suddenly dead heavy. Like it wouldn't do what she wanted. Like she'd never get her feet round those steps.

And she didn't! She was hardly on stage when she tripped and felt herself falling. She pushed frantic arms out to try to stop herself, and it went from bad to worse. She sent the girl in front of her sprawling.

'Zoe Maguire!' Amy Enright bawled as she fell onto the hard floor with a loud thwack. Cushioning Zoe, who fell on top of her.

The music played on. But the dancers were in turmoil.

Amy Enright yelled at Zoe. 'Ow! Ow! Get off! Get off me Zoe Maguire you – you – clumsy clodhopper!'

Zoe nearly died as the cry echoed round the stage and auditorium.

Amy was all arms and legs as she struggled to get up.

The dancers glared.

The conductor scowled.

But the audience cheered. They thought it was part of the act.

Then Miss Winston appeared in the wings and started waving her arms about.

'GET UP GIRLS,' she bellowed.

The audience hushed expectantly.

'GET UP AND GET ON WITH IT AS IF NOTHING'S HAPPENED!'

Amy got up. Rubbed her elbows and knees. Looked at the audience, milking it for sympathy.

Ahhh! – it responded. *Ahhh!* Going into pantomime mode.

'I'm so sorry,' Zoe whispered fiercely, getting up, and helping Amy up.

'So you should be, you clodhopper,' Amy shouted.

Zoe crumpled.

But then they were in position. The music restarted and the dance carried on – as if nothing'd happened. Except that the audience had got a taste for the slapstick and wanted more. So as they clapped enthusiastically in time to the music, they also whistled and hooted all through the dance.

It was a fiasco.

After the ordeal, subdued dancers glared at Zoe as they sat down at the back of the stage.

Zoe's shoulders slumped...

The rest of the concert passed her by in a dream, till she heard the buzz of Frankie's music.

As soon as they saw Frankie and the other two girls, the audience went wild. This they *did* want to see.

And they let them know it. Frankie was by far the best. She was brilliant. And when the dance was finished, the audience stamped their feet and roared till they did it again.

The concert was a resounding success and even Miss Winston beamed with pride and pleasure.

But back in the changing room, Frankie made a beeline for Zoe. And hanging on her arm was Amy Maguire. Amy was one of Frankie's biggest buddies.

'You ruined it for Amy,' Frankie accused Zoe.

'Made me look a right fool,' Amy said.

'Ruined it for all of us,' one of the other dancers said.

'But I've got the bruises to show it,' Amy said, rubbing her elbow.

'The audience thought it was a set-piece,' someone else said.

'They loved it. We should think about including it in every performance!' another said and burst out laughing.

One or two others saw the funny side now too.

But Frankie leaned over and eyeballed Zoe. Eyes of Every-Colour and No-Colour blazed ferociously at her. 'It was a real pantomime stunt. Don't do it again!' she warned Zoe.

Frankie needn't worry – for the other performances Zoe would make very very sure nothing like that happened again.

Zoe suddenly realised that Frankie wasn't so much looking after Amy's interest, as jealous of the attention the incident had created. Frankie wanted *her* performance to be the only thing everyone was talking about. Not Zoe's.

Well. She was welcome to the limelight. Zoe piled on her clothes and got out of school as fast as she could.

Chapter Three

The concert over, tonight there was one of several Christmas discos at school. Rules allowed students to buy tickets for one disco only, which was fair. It made for a good mix, and made sure that no one event would be over subscribed.

'Nothing,' Mel complained. 'I've got nothing to wear to the disco. It's not fair.' She emptied all her clothes onto the floor. Left them there. And it was the last Zoe saw of her.

Zoe poked through her own clothes then flopped on the bed and picked up her diary. *I've got nothing to wear either, Zara,* she wrote. Paused. *Frankie and her buddies have been on about it all week at school,* she wrote on. *Telling each other what they've bought for the disco, or what they're borrowing. And it's not just about what they're going to wear. But who'll be with who. And what they'll get up to.*

Zoe wasn't sure why she shuddered.

Dad and Mum were going to a party that night too. So they dropped Zoe off on their way. They'd told Mel to look out for her, but Mel had gone to a mate's and wasn't coming till later.

'Have fun and be good,' Mum called as Zoe got out of the car. 'But if you can't be good be careful.'

And then they laughed. The sort of laugh Zoe hated – as if her parents were sharing a joke at her expense...

She ventured into the heaving hall with her head down. Found herself a corner. Glanced furtively round. Saw nothing familiar.

Everything reminding her it was the school hall had vanished. Replaced by vast posters painted by the sixth form art class that seemed to jump off the walls. Huge blocks of colour. Lines that crossed and crisscrossed each other. Distorted faces. Headless figures and weird shapes.

Multi-coloured lights were rotating and flashing from the ceiling, distorting the images and making everyone look as if they were from another planet. Music boomed and bounced off every surface.

Kids were already dancing. On their own in a world of their own. Self consciously in pairs. Or showily in gangs. Groups of girls dancing together. Groups of boys too. Interpreting the music in as many different ways as there were colours on the walls.

Zoe stood. Watching. On her own. Shivering with anxiety.

It *feels as bad as my first day at Chapel Street Senior, Zara.*

Zoe remembered her first day here as clearly as if it were yesterday. How worried she'd been. Zoe hated first times at anything. She liked things to be familiar. Familiar was – safe.

Then she spotted Frankie in the centre of a group of dancers, doing a repeat performance of the concert dance. Others were joining in, copying the snakelike movements. Tonight she was wearing a skinny black T-shirt with cut outs, and skin-tight black trousers with cut outs too. Exposed patches of flesh were covered in glitter which caught the lights as she moved. And her hair, now jet black to match the outfit, glittered as it spun round her head. She looked stunning.

As others joined in and others stopped to watch, the group became the centre of attention and Frankie the star.

Feeling inadequate in her pink trousers and top, Zoe went closer. But stiffened when Frankie spotted her and danced up to her. 'Managing to stay on your feet?' she yelled over the music. And laughed.

The music stopped and the group began to disperse.

'On your own?' Frankie said sarcastically.

Like it was a sin.

Zoe cringed. 'My best friend couldn't come,' she blurted out.

Frankie tossed her head. 'So who is she, then? This best friend?' she said challengingly. As if she knew Zoe was lying.

'Zara,' Zoe said, without thinking. Then drew in her breath. She hadn't meant to mention Zara.

'And who is she then, this Zara?' Frankie asked.

Like Zara was the pits.

Zoe wasn't having that. 'She's been my best friend for ages,' she said – after all, didn't Frankie think she was everybody's best friend? – 'We see each other all the time. We're always together. She goes to the Ellis School over the other side of the estate,' she said.

That hooked Frankie. Everyone at Chapel Street Senior was interested in what went on at the Ellis School. Rivalry between the two schools was intense.

'Pity she couldn't have come tonight then. Keep you company,' Frankie said sarcastically. 'But I suppose she'd think she was too good for us anyway.'

'Course she wouldn't. She'd have loved it. She's very popular. Like you Frankie.'

That went down well. Frankie was used to and expected flattery. She smirked at Zoe.

Andy Raine, who was in their class, suddenly walked up to them and flashed his toothy grin. He stared admiringly at Frankie and Frankie gave him the eye back. Zoe wished she could do that. When Andy looked at her she just felt embarrassed. 'Your stunt at the concert was great. Really livened it up,' he said to her with another show of his uneven teeth.

Zoe didn't know what to say.

When the music started up again, Frankie shimmied provocatively onto the dance floor. And Andy followed her.

Zoe watched. Envious...

Standing. Watching. On her own. She wasn't the only one on her own. But it felt like she was.

So Zoe wandered round.

Weaving round the dancers, she saw Frankie dancing with Andy. But when Andy spotted her again he stopped dancing and wiped his brow. 'I could do with a drink, Frankie. Are you coming for a drink with us, Zoe?'

Frankie looked peeved when Zoe followed them to the bar.

All the while they were drinking their coke, she looked decidedly put out and kept giving Zoe surreptitious scowls.

And when they'd finished, and Andy asked Zoe to dance, the scowl became a look of pure venom.

But Zoe'd never been so happy in her life...

Later, on her own again, Frankie passed Zoe as she made for the door with her buddies. 'We're going for some air,' she said, and paused. Staring at Zoe.

Zoe frowned. Was it an invitation or what, she wondered?

Well. It was hot and stuffy in here. And she was lonely again. So Zoe tagged on to the end of them and followed them down the cool corridor...

When they got to a classroom door, Frankie opened it as if she was going inside. But Zoe hovered, knowing classrooms were out of bounds tonight.

The next thing she knew, however, she was being manhandled into the classroom to the accompaniment of catcalls.

And then the door slammed shut.

Zoe heard a scuffling noise. She tried to open the door but it wouldn't budge. Something was blocking it.

She heard footsteps running down the corridor. And laughter.

The empty classroom was big and gloomy. And it was scary in here on her own.

How was she going to get out? How long would

she have to stay in here? If she shouted, would anybody hear her over the music?

She slipped down onto the floor and curled up into a ball. *What am I going to do, Zara?* she whimpered.

Chapter Four

What seemed like for-ever-later, Zoe heard something being moved. The door opened and Frankie stood there on her own.

She held the door open for her and Zoe rushed out.

She ran to the cloakroom and got her coat. She'd had enough of the disco. She ran out of school. Ran all the way home.

The house was empty. Tod on a sleep over. Mum and Dad at the party. Mel at the disco, she supposed.

Zoe dragged off her clothes and jumped into bed.

What's the matter with everyone? she said and she punched and punched her pillow...

'What happened to you? Did you get off with someone then? I looked everywhere for you,' Mel said the next morning.

Zoe pretended to be asleep.

'I know you're awake, Zoe. So you may as well tell me what happened. I'll find out anyhow.' She pulled on jeans and T-shirt, applied hair gel, then spent the next five minutes in front of the mirror teasing her hair into shape. 'So?' she finally said.

'It was a bore. I came home,' Zoe mumbled.

'What was it like then?' Mum asked over breakfast.

'Zoe says it was a bore,' Mel said with a sniff.

'That's cos *she's* a bore,' Tod said, his mouth full of toast.

'Mind your own,' Zoe said, making herself busy with the cereal packet.

'Come on, tell us all about it,' Mum said.

'It was boring,' Zoe said.

Mum got up.

'Just because you don't know how to enjoy yourself doesn't mean something's a bore. It was great,' Mel said gulping a mouthful of tea.

'You always enjoy yourself. Hedonist!' Zoe said. Pleased for remembering the word.

'Language!' Tod said. Thinking it sounded like a swear word.

'You've got to loosen up a bit. Learn to enjoy yourself,' Mel said.

'She don't know how to. That's her trouble,' Tod said.

'And we all know how you enjoy yourself,' Zoe said. 'And how it always ends in trouble.'

'Do you good to get into a bit of trouble,' Tod snapped.

Zoe grabbed her bowl and went upstairs.

And it was the same at school on Monday. The classroom heaved with excited gossip about the disco. Zoe wondered if it included juicy details about her. But at least Frankie kept her distance. And Zoe kept shtum...

She was glad on Wednesday of that week when term ended.

Another term over, she wrote in her diary that night. And then gulped. Thinking about how a succession of days accumulated into weeks. And a term. Time dripping slowly away. Like water. Water filling a bowl. Then a bath. And suddenly a reservoir. *Time passing me by, Zara...*

...Like the Christmas holidays – which slipped uneventfully by for Zoe, who occupied herself by getting stuck into the project they'd been given for homework.

Mel was out with her mates most of the time. And Tod was his usual self, getting into scrapes. Mr Jones next door, asked him to stop lobbing the football into his garden. And the next time Tod did it he refused to give the ball back. Dad and Mr Jones nearly came to blows about it. Then Tod tormented Mr Jones by using the front of his house for his skateboard. Mr Jones didn't appreciate that either.

While Mum looked continually frazzled. 'I shall be glad when you're all back at school, and we're at work,' she said.

Spring term will be better than the Christmas term, Zoe wrote in her diary towards the end of the holiday. *Less distractions. More emphasis on work. That will suit me.*

But she was wrong about that. Because Valentine's Day loomed large on the agenda for some, almost from the beginning of term.

Everyone liked Mrs Ruskin their form teacher. You could always have a joke and a laugh with her. One morning, there was a mischievous gleam in her eyes.

'Miss Grear's doing a Valentine's Day Assembly next week,' she told them.

There was an expectant hush.

'The theme, Valentine cards,' she said, barely concealing a grin.

'I shouldn't think she knows much about them. Nobody'd send her one, Miss,' Andy Raine called out.

Everyone laughed, but Mrs Ruskin gave Andy one of her shrivelling looks. 'Miss Grear would like cards sent to her for her assembly,' she continued. – 'Not sent to her personally, that is,' giggles interrupted her – 'but sent *via* her as it were.'

'What's got into her, then?' Kevin Kingdom muttered, his gruff, recently acquired baritone voice carrying round the room.

Mrs Ruskin put her head on one side and gave him the eye too. Then she carried on, 'There are to be no names on the valentines of course. Miss Grear stresses anonymity.'

'It's a bit pointless then, isn't it?' Frankie said.

'I'm sure all will be revealed at the Assembly, Frankie,' Mrs Ruskin said.

'I hope not, Miss!' Andy Raine said, looking round and grinning at Frankie, who gave him the eye back.

If Mrs Ruskin was the teacher they all liked best, then Miss Grear had to be the one they liked least.

With parents it was her appearance they disliked. Miss Grear wore layers of black clothes perpetually, with flat black sandals and bare feet, all year round. So she was: "That teacher who couldn't look scruffier if she tried. What an example to set the kids!" – and that from Zoe's mum who hardly ever dressed in anything except leggings and baggy T-shirt.

But add to this Miss Grear's mass of dull black hair that everyone swore she never washed or combed, generous dollops of black eye make-up and nearly-black lipstick, and to the kids she was beyond the pale. Zoe felt a bit sorry for her. Miss Grear was a loner too. But she also found her unnerving. And she put that down to the lessons she taught, which included Personal, Social and Health Education. And that meant discussions in class about all the things that embarrassed her. While the other kids couldn't get enough of these subjects, Zoe hated them. Everybody thought they knew better than Miss Grear anyway. So she was criticised by kids and parents alike, either for saying too much or too little.

The more Zoe thought about this Valentine Assembly, the more it bothered her. She couldn't think of anything worse than having to listen to sloppy messages read out aloud and everyone trying to guess who they were meant for.

But everyone else was agog with excitement.

Valentine's Day arrived.

At home Mel was in a state. Up and dressed and waiting for the postman. When he got to the house she almost dragged the poor man inside. But he laughed it off. 'This what you're waiting for, me dear?' he said handing her a wad of envelopes.

'Cool!' she said.

They were all for her except one, which she threw at Tod hovering nearby. He grabbed the envelope and disappeared while Mel tore hers open.

Zoe wasn't expecting any, but still felt left out. *If I feel like this at home, Zara, what's it going to be like at school?*

Mum's mouth turned down as she watched Mel with the cards. 'Let's see yours then,' she said to Tod as he reappeared.

'No, it's personal,' he said prissily. 'You didn't get any then?' he said looking at Zoe. Knowing fine.

But it was Mum he upset. 'Nor me,' she said. 'All the girls at work'll have something. Flowers. Chocolates. Cards. Nothing for me.'

Dad just grinned and slapped her backside as he pushed past her on his way out to work. 'What do you want with them things when you've got me?' he said.

Mum sighed.

Zoe felt sorry for her...

But she felt even sorrier for herself when she got to school. Where, if you didn't have at least one Valentine card to boast about, it was a *major* sin. And one not to be admitted.

Zoe heard one girl confiding to her best friend that she'd bought all three of her cards for herself. Disguised the writing in each one. Bought stamps for them and posted them. And it'd worked. No one was teasing her.

Zoe wished she'd thought of it. This felt even worse than the unofficial who-got-the-most-Christmas-cards competition last term.

But thankfully most of the kids were too preoccupied to notice her.

Except Frankie.

When Zoe saw Frankie making a beeline for her, her insides tightened. She tried to move out of the way, but Frankie followed her. 'Where's your cards then?' she demanded.

'Left them at home,' Zoe lied, desperately hoping it didn't look like she was lying. 'Two.'

Frankie sniggered. 'More likely you didn't get any,' she said.

Zoe's shoulders slumped. How could anyone be so mean?

'Oh well. You might get a surprise yet,' Frankie said mysteriously.

Kids filed into the hall expectantly. And when Miss Grear walked in, a ripple of excitement swept through them. They craned their necks.

Miss Grear settled herself. Then picked up a card and read in her little girl voice, '"To Coochy Coo,"' – There were splutters all round, but Miss Grear didn't pause for breath – 'the same vocab as in my day. Very interesting...'

'Perhaps *you* wrote it then, Miss. Who's it for? Who do you fancy?' a big mouth shouted.

There was laughter.

Miss Grear's face almost cracked into a smile.

'Back to the point,' she said. '"To Coochy Coo. Are you coming out to – play – tonight?"'

Unnecessary emphasis on the word – *play*, Zoe thought.

'We all know what that means, Miss,' Big Mouth shouted again.

Miss Grear paused for the sniggers to stop, then carried on reading. '"I'll be in the usual place. Behind the bike sheds."'

Howls of laughter.

'That's the same as your day too, ain't it, Miss? My dad told me what he got up to behind the bike sheds,' Big Mouth Number Two shouted.

'Somebody's taking the mickey, Miss,' Number Three.

Miss Grear persevered. '"Can't wait. Love and kisses all over. Diddums."'

'Can't wait!'

'Diddums!'

'Kisses all over!'

School was full of big mouths today, Zoe thought.

Miss Grear let the hubbub die down. Waited for the fidgets to stop. Then waited for silence – absolute silence – before launching into one of her spiels.

And what a spiel. It was a major offensive and covered just about everything: Taking responsibility for one's emotions, Blah. Blah. Blah; Taking responsibility for one's actions, Blah. Blah. Blah; Taking responsibility for those one is involved with, Blah Blah. Blah....

'Pardon us for breathing!' someone near Zoe muttered as Miss Grear spelt out exactly what she meant and left nobody in any doubt about the point of the assembly. And all of it punctuated by significant pauses and lingering stares directed along lines of shuffling kids, who were now poking each other in the ribs and grinning at each other.

'How many cards have you had, Miss?' someone eventually interrupted her, bringing the offensive to a halt at last.

'That would be telling,' she replied coyly. And picked up and read another card.

At last Zoe noticed a little sigh and gesture which suggested Miss Grear was getting bored with the sound of her own voice. 'We'll finish with this one,' she said, picking up one last card.

Zoe sighed with relief.

'This one is curious,' Miss Grear said, her eyes roaming. '"To the One Who Fell Down, and caused a commotion on stage— "' she read.

Zoe's first thought was that Miss Grear couldn't have been at the concert or she would know who it meant. Then her heart missed a beat and her skin prickled.

Kids were staring at her.

'It's for Zoe Maguire!' someone shouted.

Zoe froze.

'No names please!' Miss Grear reminded them sharply.

Too late. Everyone was staring at Zoe.

Then Zoe caught Frankie's eye. Sitting next to Amy Enright. Both of them grinning.

Zoe's cheeks went hot.

Miss Grear put the card down quickly and said something to the effect that she wouldn't pursue this one now, as she was concerned that there was an 'agenda' to it.

There were catcalls of disapproval all round, but Zoe was grateful.

When things had simmered down, she remembered what Frankie'd said earlier. 'You might get a surprise yet!'

On the way out of the hall, Andy Raine winked at her. 'Don't let it get to you,' he said.

But it had got to her. Zoe felt wretched all that day and hated the attention that had once again been drawn to her.

At home time it wasn't over either. Because Frankie and her buddies followed her out of school.

'You can bring your *two* cards to show us tomorrow then, can't you?' Frankie said. 'We want to see them, don't we guys?'

Her buddies nodded their heads.

'You won't forget them now will you? I'll be waiting for you in the morning,' Frankie insisted.

Zoe dug her hands in her pockets and tried to brush past her but Frankie barred the way.

'Sloppy cards are they?' she asked. 'Or the suggestive type?' She put her head to one side and raised a quizzical eyebrow at Zoe.

Her followers did the same.

Zoe raised her chin. 'Well I can't bring them because there's no cards,' she said defiantly.

'Ooo-er! Get her!' Frankie said. 'Told you, didn't I?'

Zoe'd had enough. She pushed past them and raced home.

Chapter Five

The next morning, for the first time ever, Zoe didn't want to go to school.

'It's time you were up,' Mel called, as if she wasn't late herself.

'I'm not going to school,' Zoe muttered and burrowed down in the bed.

Mel came over. 'What's up with you then?' she said and thumped Zoe's bedclothes.

Zoe burrowed deeper.

'Something's up with Zoe,' Mel yelled.

Mum appeared upstairs, breathless.

'What's the matter?' she said. 'Come on, Zoe. You know I can't do with hassle in the mornings,' she said.

Hassle? It was so unfair. Zoe was usually the last one to give Mum any hassle. She flounced out of bed. The aggro was giving her a headache.

Gloomily, she pulled her school uniform on, scraped a comb through her hair, and decided to keep a low profile at school today.

Only she couldn't do that. Because Frankie was waiting for her. Just as she'd said.

But she'd told Frankie there were no cards – so what could she want, Zoe wondered?

Actually, it was Zara on Frankie's mind. 'So what about this friend of yours, this Zara?' she demanded. 'If she's as popular as you say, how many valentines did she get then?'

'Zara got tons,' Zoe answered flippantly, like it ought to sound for Frankie to believe her.

'Did they do anything special at the Ellis yesterday then?' Frankie persisted.

'Designed their own cards,' Zoe said. It was so easy to make up things about Zara. 'There was a prize for each year. And Zara won one.'

'And knowing the Ellis School, I suppose the prize was a gold star? They're all poncy at that school,' Frankie said.

'Actually it was a free pass at Ziggy's,' Zoe said off the top of her head. Pleased at the jealous look on Frankie's face. Mel was always telling Zoe that Ziggy's was the *in* place.

'Well, Zara won't be able to use it then, will she?

She's too young for Ziggy's, isn't she? They must know that at Ellis,' Frankie said suspiciously.

Zoe thought fast. 'It was the kids organised the prizes,' she said. Hoping it sounded convincing 'And anyway. Zara can easy pass for eighteen,' she added for luck.

It worked. Frankie looked decidedly huffy.

Zoe hoped it was the last she'd heard about Valentine's Day.

It was. But it wasn't the last she'd heard about Zara. Because most days now Frankie singled Zoe out and asked her about Zara.

Zoe was happy. She found herself enjoying this sort of attention. And suddenly it felt like *she* had a laugh on Frankie.

Since the Ziggy mistake, though, she was careful what she said, planning and going over in her head every night what she was going to say the next day...

'We won the table tennis last night,' she said one morning. 'Zara's brilliant. And my game's coming on.' She'd already told Frankie all about the local church youth club they both attended.

Another morning she had great fun describing a dance competition – how exciting it was right to the end when, of course, Zara won. 'She looked brilliant in her electric blue leotard and tights. The boys couldn't keep their eyes off her.'

Another morning she said, 'We went to a film last night.'

'Don't tell me. *Snow White*?' Frankie retorted. 'Or was it something more racy, like *Beauty and the Beast*?'

'Actually it was the new Bond movie,' Zoe snapped back and enjoyed the flicker of envy that crossed

Frankie's face. The movie had only opened at the cinema last night.

So. With things to talk about, Zoe became one of the in crowd. And all because of Zara.

If only Frankie knew!

But then it happened.

The worst. The absolutely worst thing that could happen to Zoe, happened.

One day Zoe stayed at school for netball practice. And when she got home, there was Frankie. Right there in her house. Waiting for her.

'I was in the area. So I thought I'd pop in on the off chance of meeting the famous Zara,' she said when Zoe got home.

Mel looked at Zoe, surprised. 'Zara?' she said.

Inside her head Zoe screamed, Please don't say anything Mel!

But Mel did say something. With a puzzled frown she said, 'I don't know any Zara, Zoe.' Then she frowned. 'That imaginary friend thing when you were a kid, though, you called *her* Zara.'

Frankie's eyebrows shot up.

The palms of Zoe's hands went clammy. She felt sick.

Frankie punched a fist into the palm of her hand,

and her shoulders shook. 'That's it!' she said. '"She's been my best friend for ages. We're always together. She goes to the Ellis School..."' she mimicked Zoe.

Zoe raced upstairs. Slammed the door shut. And stayed there till Frankie had gone.

'I didn't mean to drop you in it, Zo,' Mel said when she came upstairs and saw how upset Zoe was. 'When I told Mum and Dad, they said you finished with all that Zara thing years ago. So what's going on?'

Zoe didn't know what to say.

This time she refused to go to school and meant it.

And it worked. At first. But after the next day, and the next, even Zoe knew it couldn't go on. She had to go back sometime.

But Frankie would have told everyone about Zara.

On the way to school, Zoe was sure she was on her way to humiliation and shame.

She lingered outside the school gate till well past in-time. Then ... in the gates. Up the path. Through the doors. Along the corridors. And into the classroom...

For a moment it went quiet. Then there was a coming together of heads. Chattering. And giggling. Just as she'd thought. She was the talk of the class.

The year. The school. The universe.

Only Mrs Ruskin's arrival brought back some normality. 'Glad you're back, Zoe. You still look a bit peaky though,' she said. 'Take it easy today.' And she smiled at her.

In the next few days, Zoe found out that if she pretended she and the teacher were the only ones in lessons, she could cope. If she kept her eyes firmly on the ground moving round the school, she could cope. And if she volunteered for anything and everything at break times, she could cope. Because it kept her out of the way of the other students.

So she stayed in to water plants, sort and repair books, tidy the library, help prepare the labs, and feed the pets. Anything rather than face the others.

Mum said it would die a death. 'They'll soon forget about it, Zoe. There'll be more exciting things to gossip about at Chapel Street Senior than you. You'll see.'

And she was right.

Zoe knew things were back to normal when her classmates stopped nudging each other when she went into the room.

Even Frankie seemed to forget about it. One morning she was waiting inside the school gates, and when she saw Zoe she stopped her. Rested an arm round Zoe's shoulder.

Zoe was suspicious at first, but Frankie chatted about anything and everything. And never mentioned Zara once.

Perhaps it hadn't been such a big deal after all? Zoe thought.

The next day Frankie did the same thing.

And the next.

Things are getting better, Zoe wrote in her diary. *Frankie is nice. She's my friend now.*

The next morning Frankie took her really by surprise though. 'I'm having a sleepover at the weekend. You can come if you like, Zoe,' she said.

Zoe's mouth dropped open.

'Shut your gob then,' Frankie said, but with a laugh, making it sound friendly.

Zoe was still too shocked to answer.

'Please yourself then. Shan't ask again,' Frankie said as if she was disappointed.

But she continued to single Zoe out. And she did ask her again.

And feeling more confident at last, Zoe said yes. She'd got to the point where she badly wanted to think the best of Frankie.

That night she wrote in her diary. *It's the first time*

anyone in the class has asked me to a sleepover. And I do want to go.

Then she chewed her pen thoughtfully.

It will be all right won't it, Zara? she wrote.

Chapter Six

The next day Dad was working and Mum was out, so Frankie's dad had arranged to pick Zoe up. But as the time came for him to collect her, Zoe began to lose her nerve. She still wasn't sure about Frankie. Yet that part of her that'd agreed to, still wanted to go.

The door bell made her jump.

Zoe grabbed her bag and rushed downstairs before she had time to think any more. And she was out the door before she changed her mind.

Zoe didn't know what she'd expected Frankie's dad to be like. Except it wasn't the fat little man with the bald head and glasses who stood squinting at her on the door step.

'Zoe Maguire?' he said. 'I'm Frankie's dad.'

She must've looked surprised because he laughed. 'I

know. Frankie's friends always expect me to be something different,' he said apologetically. 'Sorry to be such a disappointment.'

'That's okay,' Zoe mumbled, liking him. She knew what it was like to be a disappointment, too.

And she didn't know what she'd expected Frankie's house to be like. Except it wasn't the terraced house with lace curtains at the window and paint peeling off the sills.

What she'd expected was a hunk of a father to die for. And a house that was – well – different.

But it made her glad she'd come. Because somehow it cut Frankie down to size.

However, Frankie's mum did live up to expectations.

She was as unique as Frankie but in a different way. The same startling eyes – except that whereas Frankie's had a blank give-nothing-away expression, Mrs James's lit up an open sunny smile. She had freckles, and wore no make-up. Blonde, straggly curls tumbled round her shoulders. And she was dressed in a simple long white crumpled dress. Plimsolls completed the childlike look.

She held her hand out to Zoe, who shook it jerkily. 'Hi, Zoe. Come in. Call me Joanne,' she said.

'Hi, Zoe,' Frankie called from the top of the stairs.

'Up you go, Zoe.' Frankie's mum stood aside and gestured to Zoe to go on up.

Zoe walked up the stairs.

'Come on in,' Frankie said.

Zoe pushed the door open. Saw Amy Enright. Looked around. Then understood...

Lilac walls were dotted with black and white photographs of hunks. The painted floor was purple. The furniture lime-green. Purple bed clothes were heaped untidily on the bed. Very up yours and Girl Power.

Except for one thing.

In the middle of the room, on a large black and white rug, there stood a miniature child-sized table, laid out with child-sized things for a tea party. And

round the table, on child-sized chairs, sat some dolls.

'We're having a tea party,' Frankie said, deadpan.

'This is Peggy,' Amy said solemnly, pointing to a doll.

'And this is Lucy,' Frankie pointed to another.

'This is Pippa,' Amy said.

'And this is Polly,' Frankie said.

Zoe wanted to back out of the door, but when she tried to move, Frankie darted round and blocked the door.

'We were going to ask Andy Raine,' Amy said, looking at Zoe knowingly. 'We know you like him Zoe. But he's besotted with Frankie,' she said meaningfully.

'Mum and Dad wouldn't let me invite him, though. Didn't trust us. I don't know why,' Frankie said innocently.

They both giggled and Zoe blushed.

'We thought you'd make up for it, though, by bringing Zara,' Frankie said.

Zoe's heart thudded.

'That's why we're having a tea party,' Amy said, innocently.

'What's Zara got to say for herself then Zoe? We want to know how it works, don't we Amy?' Large eyes stared at Zoe.

Zoe widened her eyes to keep back the tears. The back of her throat ached so she could hardly talk, but she managed to stutter, 'I-I-I want to go home.'

'Sh-sh-she wants to go home!' Amy said.

'Z-Z-Zoe wants to go home?' Frankie repeated. 'But we've not talked to Z-Z-Z-ara yet. That's not fair Zoe. Keeping Zara all to yourself.'

Amy pulled one of the small chairs away from the table. Knocked the doll off it. And Frankie put a hand on Zoe's head. 'Sit down,' she ordered and shoved Zoe's head down so hard that her knees buckled. She fell onto the tiny chair, Frankie's hand still on top of her head. Then Amy shoved her legs round and under the table. It hurt her knees.

'Now then. It's party time.'

'Pour a drink for Zara.'

Two pairs of eyes watched and waited.

Her hands shaking, Zoe picked up the teapot.

'Pour!' Frankie instructed.

Zoe poured into a cup. It was a brown liquid.

'We couldn't get any tea, Zoe. So we got vinegar instead. It's ok, it's watered down,' Frankie said as if it was the most natural thing in the world to have. 'Tell Zara to drink it.'

Zoe clamped her teeth together. They couldn't make her say anything.

'Okay. You drink it for her then,' Frankie said.

Zoe's teeth were still clamped together.

Frankie leant down till they were eyeball to eyeball. 'Drink it Zoe. Zara's thirsty.'

Frankie put the doll's cup to Zoe's mouth. She took a sip. Choked. It tasted acrid.

'Another sip. A bigger one!' Frankie ordered.

Zoe swallowed and nearly choked on the foul tasting liquid. It stung her throat and made her eyes run and took her breath as it went down. She coughed and spluttered.

'Don't you like watered-down vinegar with worcester sauce, then? And after all the trouble we went to get it?' Frankie said and grabbed Amy. They hugged each other and jumped up and down.

Zoe jumped up. The table tipped. The dolls fell off the chairs.

Then the door opened and Frankie's mum stood there.

Zoe ran past her out of the room. Down the stairs. Out of the door.

Although she was a car ride away from home she didn't care. She just wanted to be out of the house...

Chapter Seven

By the time she got home, her legs ached and her head throbbed.

She crept inside.

She was through the hall and going up the stairs when her mum called over the telly. 'That you, Zoe? I thought you were staying the night?'

Zoe ignored her and went upstairs.

Mum came up. 'What's the matter, Zoe? Why have you come home? How did you get home?'

'It was awful, Mum,' Zoe said and burst into tears.

She felt bereft. Because at that moment it felt like even Zara wasn't there for her any more.

The next morning Mel demanded to know what had happened and why she was home.

But Zoe couldn't talk about it.

'I'll get that Frankie,' Mel threatened.

But Zoe didn't want any more trouble. She just wanted to keep herself to herself.

This time, when she refused to go to school yet again, Dad had something to say about it. 'I don't know what's going on at *that place*,' he said. 'But I'm going to find out!'

To Zoe's dad, school was always *that place*.

'I'm taking you there myself, right now,' he said. 'And I'm going to find out what's upsetting my girl.'

Zoe was glad of his sympathy. But the last thing she wanted was Dad going up to school and losing his temper. So she told him she felt much better. Really. There was no problem. Really.

On the way to school, it occurred to her to bunk off. But where would she go? What would she do? She was too used to doing the right thing to fill a whole day doing something she shouldn't be doing.

So. Once again Zoe found herself on the way to school. And dreading it.

But Frankie and Amy behaved perfectly normally when they saw her. Frankie ignoring her altogether now. Perhaps she'd finally had her fun, and that was that, Zoe thought. Anyway, it suited Zoe fine. She preferred being invisible again. It was best this way.

Then one morning Mrs Ruskin told them about the field trip in the summer term. And suddenly there was something else to think about.

'This year you're privileged to be doing an Outward Bound Adventure Course,' she said. 'So there will be plenty for everybody to enjoy. You name it and you'll get the chance to do it. Canoeing. Sailing. Rock climbing. Abseiling. Orienteering,' she explained enthusiastically. 'And everything supervised by experts. So no need for anyone to panic.'

Too late – Zoe was already verging on panic. She'd never done anything like any of this before. And it all sounded so – difficult.

But she wasn't the only one who was worried. There was a loud groan from Frankie. 'I don't want to go on any Outward Bound Whatsit,' she moaned. 'I want to go to London like they did last year, Miss. Oxford St. Covent Garden. Leicester Square!'

'The Tate Modern. The British Museum. The V and A!' Mrs Ruskin retorted unsympathetically. 'We're not going to London this year, Frankie and that's that. So there's no point in grumbling about it.' She shuffled some notes on her desk. 'And if you want reasons, I can choose from many.' She read from her notes: '"Outward Bound is more than just a provider of outdoor activities, it is dedicated to personal development and is complementary to the educational curriculum." In other words, Frankie, it's character building.'

Frankie folded her arms on the table and dropped her forehead down with a groan.

'Don't worry, we'll stick together, Frankie,' Meena Kumar said. She was sitting next to Frankie.

Mrs Ruskin smiled at Meena.

But Frankie ignored her.

Mrs Ruskin scanned the rest of the class. 'It'll be fun. A chance to do things you've never done before, and might not have the chance to do again—' she said.

'And won't ever want to,' Frankie mumbled.

'—and it might inspire some of you to go onto other, bigger challenges,' Mrs Ruskin continued.

'It sounds wicked, Miss,' Andy Raine said, red in the face with pleasure.

'Dead cool, Miss,' Kevin Kingdom agreed.

Frankie lifted her head and scowled at them. Then shook her head as if to say they were pathetic. She wasn't used to being the one not in the swim of things, and looked very put out.

Well, Zoe thought, it was time Frankie knew how that felt. Perhaps this Outward Bound whatsit wasn't such a bad idea after all.

She caught Andy looking at her and smiled.

He grinned back at her.

Frankie caught the look between them and scowled.

Mrs Ruskin leaned back in her chair and folded her arms. 'I guarantee everyone will be scared at least once while they're there,' she said. 'And it's nothing to be ashamed of.'

'Who's saying anyone's scared?' Frankie retorted.

Mrs Ruskin rolled her eyes in exasperation. 'And we would like – expect – everyone to go,' she said firmly. 'Subsidies are available in cases of genuine hardship. And anyone without a valid reason who doesn't sign up can expect a home visit from me personally.'

Later that day, Zoe bumped into Mrs Ruskin in the corridor.

'Sorry, Miss,' she apologised.

'That's all right, Zoe. But if you go around with your eyes fixed on the ground you're bound to bump into people.'

Zoe's face flushed red.

Mrs Ruskin walked on, then turned round and walked back.

Zoe hadn't moved.

'Are you all right, Zoe? Is everything all right?' she asked.

Zoe felt her teacher's eyes burning into hers.

'Are you looking forward to the trip? Or would *you* rather have gone to London?'

'No, Miss,' Zoe answered truthfully.

'But you're not happy about Outward Bound either?'

Zoe bit her nails. She wished she could explain to Mrs Ruskin how anything new worried her. 'It's a bit scary, Miss,' she mumbled.

'Of course it is. Anything new is a *bit* scary.'

The way she said it, made it seem like it was the most natural way in the world to feel. Zoe's face broke into a grin.

'That's better, Zoe. The trick is to go for it,'

Mrs Ruskin said. And smiled.

But there was still the problem of funding. Zoe fidgeted from one foot to the other.

'Is something else worrying you?' Mrs Ruskin asked.

Zoe bit her nails again.

'You'll make your fingers sore,' Mrs Ruskin said.

Zoe put her hands in her pockets. 'I suppose it'll be expensive, Miss,' she said quietly.

Mrs Ruskin paused. Put her head on one side. 'Don't worry, Zoe. Something will turn up...'

Last year, when Mel wanted to go to London, you'd have thought that without the visit to the capital, she'd be blighted for life. She'd got up to all sorts of tricks to get the money.

Now it was Zoe's turn.

She waited till they were in a good mood. *Coronation Street* finished. Dad getting ready to go and watch footie down the pub. Mel hanging out somewhere. And Tod upstairs doing whatever he did up there.

Zoe took a quick breath. 'The trip next term—' she said.

Dad sighed. 'How much?' he asked, before he knew anything else about it.

'I don't know yet,' Zoe said, 'but Mrs Ruskin will be sending details soon. And she says there's subsidies available.' She explained all about the trip, trying to impress them with the character building bit. 'Mrs Ruskin says anyone who doesn't sign up will get a home visit,' she said finally. That'll be enough to shame them into letting me go, she thought, but crossed her fingers behind her back anyway.

'Subsidies, they'll be for them single mothers. They expect everything to be paid for them,' Dad said, getting wound up now. 'People like us who work for a living never get any help.'

'That's not fair!' Mel chipped in, appearing as if by magic. 'There's two of you working and it's still a struggle. Try being a single mother and see what it's like.'

'Too true there's two of us working,' Dad said. 'And don't you forget it.'

'The trip sounds wicked,' Tod said, also appearing from nowhere.

For once Zoe could have kissed him.

'Well, just let any nosey teacher come round here and stick her nose in our business and I'll tell her a few facts of life,' Dad snorted.

'Mel went to London—' Zoe wheedled.

'Thank God! You wouldn't have got me on any Outward Bound thingamajig.' Mel shuddered. 'Better if they say no to you now, Zo. Let you off the hook.'

'But I want to go,' Zoe insisted.

'Trust you,' Mel groaned.

'I'm going when it's my turn,' Tod said. 'But I don't know about our Zoe. It doesn't sound like her to me.'

'Pig!' Zoe said.

'Well you'll just have to chip in, Zoe,' Mum said. 'Get yourself a job.'

Chapter Eight

She called in at the local paper shop, but it had
nothing for her. So how else could she earn some
money? Zoe was getting desperate, when one home
time Mrs Ruskin called her back into the empty
classroom. 'Can you spare a minute, Zoe?' she said.

Zoe frowned, wondering what she wanted.

Mrs Ruskin stuffed a bundle of files into her bag,
then asked Zoe to sit down. 'Don't look so worried.
You're not in trouble,' she said.

Zoe grinned sheepishly.

'That's better. You've got a nice smile, Zoe. We
don't see enough of it though. Now. I've got a
suggestion.' She leaned her elbows on the desk, rested
her chin on her hands and looked Zoe in the eye.
'You might not know it, but I'm a busy mum as well
as a teacher.'

It'd never occurred to Zoe that teachers had the same sort of problems as other mortals. But what was it to do with her anyway?

'Does your mother work, Zoe?'

'Yes, Miss.' Zoe was more puzzled than ever. Where was this leading?

'So you know what busy lives we working mums lead?'

Zoe nodded vigorously. 'My mum says there's never enough hours in the day, Miss.'

'Exactly.' Mrs Ruskin dragged her fingers through her hair in the same way Zoe's mum did when she was stressed out. 'And one of the worst times of the day for me is right now.' Her eyes lingered on a pile of exercise books on the desk 'Marking. Reports. Tomorrow's lesson plans. And jobs waiting for me at home too.' She let out a long sigh.

'It's the pits, Miss,' Zoe said sympathetically. 'When my mum gets home she's always in a bad mood too.'

Mrs Ruskin flinched. 'I hope my children don't think I'm always in a bad mood,' she said frowning. 'That's really sad. But that's where you come in,' she said, suddenly enthusiastic.

Zoe pointed a finger at herself enquiringly.

'I live on the other side of the estate,' Mrs Ruskin continued. 'Up near the Ellis School. Do you know where I mean, Zoe?'

'Course, Miss. That's where Za—' She stopped herself in time. She didn't know what Mrs Ruskin would make of Zara. Or of her, come to that, if she knew about Zara.

'You were saying, Zoe?'

'That's where the – the shops are,' Zoe said quickly.

'Exactly.' Mrs Ruskin nodded her head.

Curiouser and curiouser. Zoe bit her nails.

Mrs Ruskin laughed. 'There's no need for that, Zoe.'

Zoe put her hands under the table.

'I'm sorry. I'll come clean, Zoe. I was wondering if you could spare me the odd hour after school? To occupy my little darlings, or do a bit of shopping for me. It would help me no end. For a fee of course. And as long as your parents approve.'

Zoe was gob smacked. It was the last thing she'd expected.

A job – working for Mrs Ruskin – and for a fee! A broad grin spread over her face. 'Thanks, Miss,' she said.

Mrs Ruskin smiled and got up. 'Right. Shall we try it for an hour, two or three days a week, after school? See how it goes? Have a talk to your parents and see what they think about it.'

Wicked! Zoe said over and over on the way home. This was far better than a stupid paper round...

'Too true it's all right! But how much is she paying you that's what I want to know? We don't want a teacher taking advantage of my little girl, do we?' Dad said.

'That's nice of your teacher. It'll be a big help,' Mum said...

But when Zoe stood outside Mrs Ruskin's house for the first time, all at once she felt paralysed with shyness.

She sucked in a quick breath and blew it out. Then sprinted up the path.
She knocked on the door. Hopped from one leg to the other and waited.

However, Mrs Ruskin was her normal matter-of-fact self, and gave her a shopping list and money as if she was setting homework.

Zoe did the shopping. Hurried back. Handed it over. It was as easy as that. And it felt great.

The next time she went, Mrs Ruskin held the door open.

'Come in and meet the little darlings, Zoe.'

They were identical twin girls.

'Four years old,' Mrs Ruskin said.

'And a half,' one of them corrected her.

'And a half. A half is very important at their age,'
Mrs Ruskin said with an amused look in her eye.

Zoe didn't know much about four year olds. She
stared at them.

They stared back at her.

'I'm Chloe,' one said.

'And I'm Rosie,' the exact copy said. 'Do you go to
Mummy's school?'

'Yes,' Zoe said with a nervous giggle. It was funny
hearing Mrs Ruskin called Mummy.

'But are you a good one or a bad one? Mummy says

68

there are some bad children at her school,' Rosie said, rolling her eyes.

'Zoe's a very good girl,' Mrs Ruskin answered for Zoe. 'But don't give too many of my secrets away, Rosie.'

Rosie clapped her hands over her mouth, hunched her shoulders and giggled.

'You'll soon be able to tell them apart, Zoe. Rosie's the curious one. She never stops asking questions,' Mrs Ruskin said.

'Why's Zoe here Mummy? What's she going to do? Why are you here, Zoe?' Rosie asked, proving the point.

Zoe giggled. 'I'm helping Mrs Ruskin,' she said.

'Why do you call Mummy Mrs Ruskin?'

'Shut up, Rosie!' Chloe said.

'You're not allowed to say "shut up",' Rosie said with wide eyes.

Mrs Ruskin put her head on one side. 'And Chloe's the cheeky one,' she said pointedly.

'*You're* cheeky, Mummy!' Chloe retorted.

Rosie grabbed Chloe but Chloe ran off with Rosie after her.

'Now you've met them you know what you're up against, Zoe. Do you think you can handle them?' Mrs Ruskin said.

Zoe wasn't sure. But didn't say so. She didn't want to lose her job already. 'Course,' she said.

The girls rushed back. One grabbed Zoe round the leg while the other tried to pull her off.

'What do they like doing, Mrs Ruskin?' Zoe said, trying hard not to fall over.

'We like *playing*. Stupid!'

Zoe guessed it was Chloe before Mrs Ruskin pounced on her. 'If you talk like that Zoe won't come back,' she said. 'Say you're sorry, Chloe.'

Chloe pouted. 'Sorry,' she said, then added quietly, 'Stupid PooPoo!'

Zoe stared in awe at the defiant four year old. But it was Rosie grabbed her sister by the shoulders. 'You're not allowed to say Stupid PooPoo!' she said, gesturing with her hands and staring into Chloe's eyes. And sounding just like her mother.

Zoe stifled a giggle.

Mrs Ruskin 'eyed' Chloe. Zoe knew that look. It was often put to good use at Chapel Street Senior.

Chloe squirmed out of Rosie's grasp, spread her arms wide, and with palms pointing heavenwards she shrugged her shoulders, then ran off.

Zoe nearly choked with laughter.

'You have to watch that one,' Mrs Ruskin said. 'But just one thing, Zoe. It could give rise to all sorts of misunderstanding if you gossiped about this at school.'

But Zoe had no intention of gossiping about it. The last thing she wanted to add to her reputation was 'teacher's pet'.

Chapter Nine

Zoe enjoyed the shopping bit of the job. But continued to approach the twins with caution.

Rosie's relentless questions proved to be cute, irritating and frequently impossible to answer. Chloe's cheek continued to dazzle her with its daring.

However, she soon began to get the measure of them, and Mrs Ruskin was always nearby to help her out as she cut out, coloured in, and read stories to the twins.

She found out that the best way of answering Rosie's questions was off the top of her head. The sillier the answer, the better it seemed to suit Rosie.

'Why's rain wet, Zoe?'

'Because it's not dry, Rosie.'

'Why isn't rain dry, Zoe?'

'Because it's wet, Rosie.'

'Why's the sky blue, Zoe?'

'Because it's not green, Rosie.'

'Why isn't the sky green, Zoe?'

'Because it's blue, Rosie.'

And she found out that with Chloe's cheek, it was best to reply in kind.

'You're a big cheat, Zoe,' Chloe said when Zoe won at snap.

'But you're a bigger one, Chloe,' Zoe retorted. Chloe shrugged.

'Your trainers are disgusting, Zoe,' Chloe said one day.

'And your flip flops smell, Chloe,' Zoe replied.

Chloe dragged her flip flops off and smelt them. 'Poo!' she said, then put them back on and carried on playing.

'You handle them well, Zoe,' Mrs Ruskin said one day. 'Have you ever thought of a career in child care? Teaching? A nanny? Lots of nannies travel the world.'

It sounded good to Zoe.

As the field trip drew nearer, Zoe's head was full to bursting.

Sleeping in a dormitory, Zara, she wrote in her diary one day. *I wonder who I'll share with? Will I manage the activities? I hope I don't make a fool of myself.* At another time she wrote, *It's going to be great fun. Midnight feasts. And camp fires.*

With tests over and the trip imminent, the class went into overdrive. All pretence at work was forgotten. All they could talk about was the coming trip.

The teachers didn't seem to mind, but some of them had serious difficulty keeping the lid on.

In her last lesson before the great event, Miss Grear scrawled on the board:

Getting Carried Away by the Occasion

and proceeded to address the issue at length. Then she wrote the warning:

A moment of snatched thrill can and does change lives for ever.

'I don't suppose she ever got carried away with anything except moaning,' Frankie complained.

In fact Frankie was about the only one, now, not getting carried away with excitement.

It's a dead give away. Frankie's very quiet at the moment, Zoe wrote in her diary. *She's definitely not looking forward to the trip. I bet if it wasn't for the fact she might be missing out on something, she'd have got out of it.*

Zoe, despite misgivings, was now most definitely looking forward to it.

However, on the day of the trip, she was still a bag of nerves.

As was her mum.

'I've got everything I need, Mum,' Zoe insisted for the umpteenth time.

Their neighbours, who were regular campers, had lent her a rucksack and waterproofs.

'That's everything. I'm ready now, Mum.'

Zoe hated goodbyes.

Mum grabbed her and gave her a hug.

And Dad.

Tod looked peeved. 'Wish it was me,' he said.

Mel shook her head. 'Thank God it's not me,' she said.

When they dropped Zoe off at the school car park, her parents were making her really nervous. Zoe was glad when they had to go to work. She watched other kids being dropped off.

Tearful parents and embarrassed kids.

Tearful kids and embarrassed parents.

Parents clinging onto kids as if they wouldn't let them go.

Parents dropping kids off and scarpering.

One dad cracked a joke. 'A week's peace. Phew! We've waited all his life for this.'

Mr Wright, PE teacher, was going with them. 'It'll be the making of them,' he was saying to anxious

parents, wagging a finger at them to convince them, like he always did, before turning to wink at the kids.

Miss Arnold, history teacher, was going with them. Affectionately known as Arny. Picture of efficiency with her clip board and pencil at the ready for any last minute hiccups.

But Miss Grear going with them? Now that was a surprise.

'Nobody said she was coming with us!' Kevin Kingdom's gravelly baritone pierced the hubbub.

'You didn't let on you were coming, Miss,' Meena Kumar said.

Miss Grear shrugged.

Then Mrs Ruskin arrived to see them off. 'Sorry I can't come with you, kids. But my little darlings would miss me too much.'

'You could've brought them with you,' Andy Raine shouted.

Zoe smiled secretively. They might have got more than they bargained for with Rosie and Chloe.

Frankie was one of the last to arrive. Meena Kumar ran up to her. 'Can I sit with you on the bus, Frankie?' she asked.

Frankie's bad temper was in evidence as she shrugged at Meena off-handedly. Then she sidled up to Mrs Ruskin. 'Oxford Street. Covent Garden. Leicester Square,' she said through tight lips.

'The Tate Modern. The British Museum. The V and A!' Mrs Ruskin replied with a sunny smile.

'Well even they'd be better than what we've got lined up,' Frankie said. She was in a foul mood.

There was a huge cheer as the bus pulled into the car park.

Zoe's heart lurched.

Here we go, Zara, she said.

Chapter Ten

Zoe's eyes darted anxiously round the bus, and her hands felt clammy as she pushed her way down the crowded aisle. It was like a test. If she found someone to sit with, the rest would be all right.

But kids blocked her way and progress along the aisle was difficult. And it was soon obvious that most seats were already taken.

Zoe came to a halt. She clamped her hands in her arm pits and her shoulders sagged. Then a voice piped up from somewhere. 'There's a seat here.'

Zoe looked round and located Andy Raine grinning at her. Then he did a sideways nod of his head at the empty seat next to him. Zoe smiled at him shyly. Everything was suddenly more than all right!

'Come and sit with us if you're on your own, Andy. We'll make room for you,' Frankie shouted from the back seat.

Too late. Zoe had already slumped gratefully down next to him.

Mrs Ruskin stepped up into the bus to do a head count and say goodbye. 'Quiet!' she yelled.

'Steady on, Miss, we thought Miss Winston had got on,' Kevin Kingdom yelled back.

'Well if I hear you're not behaving, Kevin – or anyone else—' Mrs Ruskin said, 'I'll send Miss Winston along to sort you out post-haste.'

There was uproar on the bus. 'You wouldn't do that to us, Miss!' Matthew Baker said, in mock horror.

'Just try me, Matt,' Mrs Ruskin said. 'So. Settle yourselves down quickly please. And if you can contain yourselves a little longer, keep quiet while I do a head count.'

At the back, Frankie and her buddies straddled the seat. When Mrs Ruskin reached them she leaned over Frankie. 'If you just let yourself, Frankie, you could end up actually enjoying yourself,' she said.

Meena Kumar grinned at Mrs Ruskin. 'She'll be all right, Miss.'

But Frankie pulled a face. 'Speak for yourself, Meena,' she said with a bad-tempered toss of her head.

Mrs Ruskin walked back along the bus, then stood and looked down its length. 'And so—' she smiled.

'Let me just say that on your return I expect to be teaching a class of newly honed super-mortals!'

'No hope of that, Miss – whatever they are,' someone yelled.

'Well. Anyway. I can't wait to hear all about it,' Mrs Ruskin said. 'Have a great time everybody,' she called as she got off the bus.

There was a loud cheer as the driver pulled out of the car park.

Andy was a chatterer.

For the whole of the journey he either leaned forward, chattering through the gap in the middle of the seat to the kids in front, or turned round and did the same to those behind him.

Zoe's head-swivelling efforts to keep up with him wore her out, but she was flushed with excitement. It was like all the day trips she'd ever been on rolled into one, and then some more.

Songs echoed up and down the aisles. Jokes rattled non-stop off the tips of tongues. Frankie, though, was noticeable for her lack of enthusiasm. Usually upfront and Leader-of-the-Gang, today she was subdued, and did her best to sabotage the good humour of the rest of them.

However, the rest of them were having none of it.

'Give it a rest, Frankie,' Kevin Kingdom yelled when she trashed another of his jokes.

'Yeah. Yeah. Give it a rest, Frankie,' the others chorused.

But Frankie wasn't used to the brush-off. 'Mind your own!' she yelled, going purple with rage.

Three hours later they swung off the road into a long winding drive.

Kids peered out of steamy windows.

'Flippin' heck!' Andy said as a huge stone building came into sight. 'Flippin' heck!'

Zoe thought it looked like the set of an old-fashioned black and white film. The sort her mum drooled over. She expected a horse-drawn carriage to dash past at any minute.

Kids leapt up and began to push forward, but Miss Arnold beckoned them back.

Mr Wright rushed to the front. 'Sit down everybody,' he yelled full-on.

Everyone sat down again.

'Is this it then, Sir?' Matthew Baker asked.

'Well if it isn't we're in big trouble, Matt,' Mr Wright said.

Everyone laughed.

Matt dropped his head and clasped his hands round the back of his neck.

Zoe felt for him. She was always saying daft things like that.

'Now. We'll get off in an orderly way,' Mr Wright said, wagging a warning finger. He always treated kids like he expected them to do the opposite to what he said, but actually had the knack of getting them to do exactly that. 'Then we wait for the driver to unload the luggage. All of it. Nobody goes anywhere till everyone has their luggage...'

At last they were inside and having a snack.

Then they were shown round. Finally they went to the dormitories.

As the girls trooped along the corridor with Miss Arnold, Zoe's heart thudded and her breathing was rapid. Finding someone to share a dormitory with was the next test. And one that had been worrying her for some time. Classmates had been chopping and changing their minds about it for weeks. Right now several girls were clutching each other to make sure they weren't separated.

Zoe wished she had a best friend.

When Miss Arnold stopped, the girls swarmed round her.

'The numbers,' she said 'fall nicely into groups of four.' She smiled reassuringly. 'And I'm going to leave you to sort yourselves out. Any difficulties, come and fetch me. My room's there at the other end of the corridor.' Her eyes lingered on them for a moment. 'But as this week's all about teamwork, I hope I won't be needed.'

As she walked off, girls disappeared through doors like magic. Leaving Zoe in the corridor alone.

She clenched her fists and straightened her back. Then took a deep breath and put her head round the first door.

Four beds. Four girls.

She tried the next dormitory. It was full too.

And the next...

Zoe opened the last door. And saw Frankie. And Amy. Faye Cooper made three. Leaving one bed spare.

Frankie saw Zoe. 'Make way for Zoe. And Zara too of course,' she added, grinning. Zoe's heart sank. As she walked slowly over to the spare bed and dropped her bag on it, it felt like the trip was now spoiled.

Chapter Eleven

A bell sounded and Miss Arnold's voice called them to meet downstairs in the lounge.

Zoe sat down unhappily on the edge of a chair.

Frankie sank back into a sofa. And when Miss Grear got out a register, she sniped, 'it's as bad as being at school.'

Miss Grear sent a sharp glance in her direction. 'It's not a bit like being at school,' she said. 'But there have to be some checks. And making sure everyone's in the right place at the right time is one of them. So get used to it now, Frankie.'

Frankie mumbled something under her breath as the register was called.

Then Mr Wright asked, 'Is everyone happy with their billet, then?'

Zoe bit her lip. There were no spare beds left

anyway – so what could she say?

'Can I change, Sir?' Meena Kumar suddenly said. 'I wanted to share with Frankie.'

Zoe was so deep in misery, the words didn't register at first.

Miss Arnold pushed her hair behind one ear as if she didn't want to know.

Miss Grear looked stony.

'Really, Meena,' Mr Wright said.

Then it hit Zoe what Meena had said.

'I'll change with you, Meena!' she said breathlessly. 'I don't mind changing with her, Sir.' *Pleeee-ase*, she begged inwardly.

Miss Grear nodded.

Miss Arnold's face softened. 'Good for you, Zoe.'

Mr Wright shrugged. 'You're in luck then, Meena,' he said. He put a thumb up at Zoe. 'You and Meena can do a straight swap and everybody's happy.'

Were they just! Zoe could've kissed Meena. Not only had she got what she wanted, but she'd earned some brownie points too.

More relaxed now, Zoe stared round the room. At the large worn sofas. The huge floor cushions. The comics and magazines littered on coffee tables. And the blocks of photographs on the walls. Curious, she got up and went to look at the photographs.

Kids astride rocky peaks. Kids abseiling down sheer rock faces. Kids negotiating the river on strange-looking rafts. Kids paddling canoes – and all of them with the same look of rapture on their faces.

But was she up to any of this? Zoe breathed heavily.

The door opened and a young guy strode in. Muscles bulged through his trendy sports gear. His face was weather tanned. His streaked-blond hair was tousled. Everyone gawped. 'What a hunk!' Frankie said.

'Welcome. I'm Pete. Your co-ordinator,' he said and perched himself down on the edge of a coffee table. Then he stared at them. 'This week's going to be a challenge to everyone in this room. You!' He pointed a finger at Andy Raine, who grinned back at him. 'And you. And you.' He pointed randomly round the group.

'Mr Wright the Second,' Kevin Kingdom's gravelly voice commented.

Mr Wright wagged a finger at Kevin and they all laughed.

'As your teachers will be doing the same things as you, it's going to be a challenge to them too,' Pete said. 'And it's *always* a challenge for us at the Centre, because no matter how many groups we deal with, each one is different. Bringing different skills.

Different strengths. Different ideas.'

Kids stared at each other, at their teachers, then back at Pete.

'Successful teamwork,' Pete said, ticking off one finger. 'That's the key to being here. Me and the staff will help all we can. We're here to teach and encourage you. But it's up to each one of you,' – he pointed again – 'working individually, but also as the member of a team, to make the week the success it should be.'

He paused, and no one broke the silence.

'Personal achievement—' he resumed, ticking off a second finger. 'That's the aim. Every one of you doing things you've never done before. And, hopefully, doing them to the best of your ability.'

His eyes glistened with enthusiasm. But then he grinned boyishly.

'Don't look so solemn, though. Because enjoyment—' he ticked off a third finger. 'That's the most important thing on the agenda.'

There were relieved sighs and grunts of approval all round.

Pete leaned back, folded his arms and kicked his leg idly against the table leg, while his eyes roamed the room. 'We staff can do our bit, but it's your input that counts,' he said finally.

Kids and teachers looked shyly round at each other.

Frankie rolled her eyes at Pete. 'I'm ready for anything, Pete,' she said breathlessly. Looking enthusiastic for the first time since she'd left school.

Meena laughed. 'You've changed your tune, Frankie.'

'So.' Pete stood up, hands on hips.

Backs straightened immediately.

'So!' he said again. 'A few activities to whet your appetites, eh?'

There were excited cheers.

'A sample of what to expect in the next few days?'

More cheers.

As Pete made for the door, everyone followed. Like he was the Pied Piper.

They found themselves outside in a sort of playground. Dotted round it were various marked-off areas and different pieces of equipment.

'This is the courtyard. Scene of many noble feats and exploits. So! Are you ready?' Pete yelled.

'Yessss!' came the answering chorus.

For the next few crazy hours, they ran, jumped, hopped. Dived in and out of obstacles. Over hurdles and under them, and through barriers. On their own. In pairs. In a group. It was fast. Funny. And very, very exciting. Everyone was caught up in it.

Even Frankie. Who, when she wasn't tagging along with Pete, tagged on to Andy Raine. Who, Zoe noticed, was only too willing to help her.

When Pete blew a whistle everyone fell to the ground, collapsing in a heap.

'Do you think you're going to enjoy yourselves, then?' he yelled.

The 'Yessss!' was an explosion of sound. Followed by more roughhousing and rolling on the ground.

Pete took the teachers on one side. 'The bonding session over!' he said. 'They're like putty in our hands now.' He looked back at the kids and grinned, then continued talking to the teachers. 'As we're the experts here, leave the work to us. You'll find that this

is a unique chance to observe your pupils.'

Mr Wright grinned. 'It sounds good,' he said enthusiastically.

'Join in with the fun with them,' Pete said, 'and I guarantee at the end of the week you'll see your students in a new light.'

He looked at the kids and grinned.

'But before we turn in for the day, let's have a photo call,' he called. 'Everyone get over there, by the wall. Squash up. We don't want anyone left out, do we?'

Everyone huddled close.

'Sausages!' Pete called.

'Sausages!' they yelled, as buckets of water were tossed over the wall at them!

Shouts of dismay and fury, breathless screams, and helpless laughter, sounded all around.

Miss Grear looked like a cat that had drowned. Black hair stuck to her head in strands so you could see white scalp through it. Black make-up was running down her face. But she wiped her face and jumped up and down with the rest of them good naturedly.

Miss Arnold, soaked, looked smaller than ever and just like one of them.

Mr Wright shook his fists at Pete.

Pete doubled up with laughter. 'It never fails!' he crowed.

There was just enough time to dry off before dinner at six thirty. Someone showed them the drying rooms where they deposited their wet clothes. Then, still laughing, they went in to eat.

For dinner, there was soup with hunks of fresh crusty bread and dollops of butter. Sausage and mash and thick onion gravy. Followed by sticky buns.

All of them everyone's favourites.

Zoe found herself head-turning again to keep up with the conversations that flowed around the long table.

She'd only been here a few hours but she was now feeling fantastic. Even after the fright over the dorm. And the dousing with water. It was funny. At home, she always felt sort of isolated. Lonely. The outsider. *And* at school. But here, it felt like the opposite. Here, she was one of the crowd.

Anita Patel, narrow dusky face dominated by her unusual misty-blue eyes, was sitting next to Zoe. And Anita's best friend, Natalie Yates, chubby cheeks dimpling as she ate, was sitting next to her. Andy Raine, his seriously funny face looking like he was angry but always breaking into a laugh, sat opposite Zoe. Frankie next to him.

The more she was getting to know Andy, the nicer he seemed.

And it seemed like Frankie felt the same. She was all over him during dinner.

'You need to stock up on energy,' Pete said as he wandered round. 'If you don't eat properly you won't stay the course.'

He needn't have worried. Plates were emptying fast.

'And sleep is as important as food – so forget about the midnight feasts – for tonight at least!'

'Thanks, Zoe,' Meena said later, as they went up to the dorms to swap their things over.

'You're welcome,' Zoe said. With feeling.

Later still, when they turned in, tiredness swept over Zoe. But it was a nice tiredness. She looked round the dormitory. Not sharing with Mel. Which felt strange. And not with Frankie. Thank goodness! It felt so good.

Natalie and Anita were huddled on a bed, gossiping.

Miriam Watson lay curled up in the other bed, covers up round her ears.

'She's homesick,' Anita said.

Zoe undressed and jumped into bed. 'Night Miriam,' she said and dived under the bedclothes too. Wondering what the next day would bring.

Chapter Twelve

In her dreams she was first and best at everything. And when she woke the next morning she felt ready for anything. And nothing!

Please don't let me be the only one who makes a fool of myself, Zara, she scribbled in her diary.

Then she pulled on shorts, T-shirt, and track suit. Brushed her hair. Checked in the mirror. Hair shining. Eyes bright. And skin glowing.

Not bad!

She hurtled down the stairs with the others, two, three, four steps at a time.

Crockery clattered and voices echoed round the dining room. But there was tension in the room this morning, too. A mixture of excitement, nervous energy, and uncertainty.

'Eat a good breakfast,' a guy was advising them as he walked round. 'You're going to need plenty of fuel to stoke the engines up today. My name's Gary, by the way, and I'll be supervising you today.' He was tall and lanky. All wrists and elbows and knees. With balding head and pale skin, he couldn't have looked less like Pete. Zoe didn't think he looked the outdoor type. Couldn't imagine him doing anything like an assault course.

'Looks like he should take his own advice. It looks like a square meal wouldn't hurt him,' Frankie muttered to no one in particular as she gulped down black coffee and refilled her mug.

Gary stared at Frankie's empty plate. 'You need food inside you this morning. Carbohydrate. And lots of it,' he said curtly.

Miss Arnold delivered a You're-Letting-the-Side-Down stare at Frankie. 'I agree with Gary,' she said. 'You must eat something, Frankie.'

'It's like the flippin' Gestapo!' Frankie complained. 'Coffee's all I ever have in the morning. It gets me going, Miss.'

'Be it on your head, then,' Gary said.

Frankie's head wobbled from side to side. 'Be it on your own head,' she repeated.

But everyone else tucked into the cereal, fruit, baked

beans on toast, and more toast that was available.

'And drink plenty, too. There'll be blood, sweat and possibly tears today,' Gary said with a lopsided grin. 'And we don't want anyone getting dehydrated. Milk's best,' he said and as if to convince them, downed a carton of milk in one. 'But anything liquid will do.' He wiped his mouth with the back of his hand.

'You don't mind if I have another coffee then, do you?' Frankie said.

Miss Arnold sighed.

Today was nominated for water activities.

First, Gary gave them a pep talk about water safety. He wanted to know who, if anyone, didn't swim. And if anyone had a fear of water – which no one admitted to. Then they were kitted out with lifejackets and safety helmets and told to meet in the courtyard...

As they walked down to the river, Zoe thought so this was it then – the adventure was beginning at last...

She tried to steady herself as she stepped into the canoe. But it bobbed up and down to the flow of the river, and it took all her time just to sit down in it.

She hadn't realised how small a canoe was. How wobbly. How fragile.

'Right,' Gary said. And demonstrated.

In the canoe. Roll. Back up.

He did a perfect flip.

Zoe gasped. Oh – was that all? She did her best not to panic. Tried to forget how much she hated first times at anything. Hesitated.

Gary was immediately by her side. He waited for her to look at him, then held her gaze. 'You can do it,' he said quietly. And his eyes said she could. His quiet confidence not only made her want to do it, but made her feel she *could*. Zoe was ashamed of how she'd judged him earlier.

'Roll!'

The canoe lurched, and she was in the water. Water in her face. Water in her ears. Water in her mouth.

Can't see! Can't breathe! Struggling, Zara!

Then. Flip! And the canoe righted itself.

She laughed hysterically. 'Easy peasy!' she spluttered.

'I knew you could do it. Good kid,' Gary said.

The others clapped.

When Gary transferred his attention to Frankie, Zoe saw a look on Frankie's face she'd never seen before. From Leader-of-the-Gang, she'd suddenly become Little-Girl-Lost.

'You can do it, Frankie,' Gary said. But Frankie wouldn't even look at him, let alone listen to him.

Zoe wanted to tell her – *Look at him Frankie* – then she'd do it, too. She opened her mouth – but Frankie got in first.

'What are you opening your gob for, Zoe Maguire?' she said, tight-lipped.

Zoe closed her mouth.

The group's attention was riveted on Frankie – something she usually loved – but not now. Not like this.

'I can't do it,' she said hoarsely.

'Oh yes you can!' Zoe said fiercely. ' If I can do it, you can.'

'Well spoken, Zo,' Andy said.

Zoe'd meant it to spur Frankie on, but Frankie directed a look of hatred at her now.

In the end it took the full effort of Gary supervising, coaxing, and supporting her, before she'd do it. And as the canoe finally went over, there was a gurgling, watery gasp from Frankie.

It seemed an age before the canoe bobbed up again and she came spluttering back to the surface. 'That's the-the-the worst piggin' thing I've ever done in my life!' she gasped, choking and coughing out water.

Smugness was a feeling Zoe wasn't used to...

The rhythmic, repetitive action as she paddled up river suited Zoe's new-found confidence.

Preparing her for the slalom course.

Followed by the races...

And afterwards, as she jumped back onto dry land, she grabbed Andy. 'Wasn't it great, Andy?' she blurted out.

Andy hugged her.

Frankie saw them – and if looks could kill! But for once, Zoe didn't care. It didn't matter that she hadn't won any of the races. Or how many poles on the slalom course she'd hit. She'd enjoyed herself, and that was everything.

After a packed lunch it was time for the raft-building.

They were put into teams. Then, with the materials provided, each team had to build a raft, and cross the river and back. First back got the team award.

Every member of the team had to help build the raft, but no one would be forced to board it if they didn't feel confident. Even the thought of having to swim the river didn't worry Zoe though. She could do anything today.

In Zoe's team there was her, Miriam, Andy, Kevin, and Mr Wright, who was more like one of them than a teacher today.

'Wet ropes knot better and don't stretch so much,' Kevin told them. He was a scout, he said, so knew about such things.

They listened to him appreciatively. Dunked the ropes in the river. Then lashed the pieces of wood and the tin drums together.

First this idea. Then that. On they worked. And on. Too busy to notice what the other teams were up to.

Kevin was definitely Leader. And Mr Wright was happy to be led.

The end result was a Weird-But-Wonderful-Raft that was hopefully river-worthy.

'Let's go for it now!' Kevin said. And they all helped to drag it into the water.

Out of the corner of her eyes, Zoe saw Frankie on the fringe of her group. Uncooperative. Hunched up. Miserable.

So now she knows what it feels like, Zara, she wrote in her diary later.

Their raft was launched. It went well. Only two on board. Kevin and Mr Wright. But the rest of the team cheering them on like mad.

They got to the centre of the river; reached the other side; no time wasted on the turn. On the way back; more confident now; paddling faster than ever.

But Miss Grear's team was close behind them and gaining. And she was on board red-faced and going crazy. Zoe couldn't believe it was her.

Nearly back.

BACK.

'We've done it. We're first!' Mr Wright punched his fist in the air. Followed by hand-slapping and hugs all round. Andy's hug was the second of the day. Zoe looked round to see if Frankie had noticed. But Frankie was nowhere to be seen.

'Well done.' Gary congratulated them, then shook everyone's hand as they got their certificate.

Zoe was ecstatic.

On the way back to the Centre, Zoe was tired but elated. And it was the best feeling ever.

After showering, they got into dry clothes for the first time since the morning.

For dinner that night it was meat pie, mash, and mushy peas. 'Keep the bed clothes well down tonight!' Andy called out and everyone laughed. Apple crumble and custard was for afters.

'Wish my mum did meals like this,' Matt Baker said.

'Do you hear that?' Pete called through the hatch to the kitchen.

Angie, the cook, popped her head through and waved.

After dinner, everybody crashed out in the lounge, where events of the day were told and retold with ever increasing exaggeration. After which they had a film show about tomorrow's activities.

And that's when real worries and excitement gripped everybody.

Much later that night, Zoe couldn't sleep. Anita and Natalie were still awake too.

Suddenly Anita flashed a torch at Zoe. 'Shall we get out some grub?' she said.

The next thing all four girls were scrabbling around for goodies. Then they sat on top of Anita's bed, a supply of sweets and goodies spread out before them.

'I couldn't sleep,' Anita said.

'Nor me,' Natalie said.

Anita asked Natalie, 'Are you nervous about tomorrow then?'

Natalie pulled a face. 'Yes,' she said, and then they grabbed hold of each other.

'Are you nervous, Zoe?' Miriam asked.

Zoe nodded.

All she could think about was that she would be the only one who couldn't do it.

Chapter Thirteen

Next morning Zoe woke up with an excitement bordering on terror.

But with the sun streaming through the window, and with yesterday's success firing her up, she felt far more determined than she'd felt in the night. After all, she'd surprised herself so far hadn't she? So as she dressed, she decided to wait and see what the day brought.

Because today was the event everyone was either dreading, or longing to have a go at.

If canoeing seemed scary, this would be mega-scary. If the trip was a test of their skills, this would be the thing that would prove them. And if the trip was a test of their nerves, this was the thing that would test them to the limit.

The Big One.

Rock Climbing. Followed by ABSEILING!

As she got on the bus taking them to the site, Zoe was pleased and flattered that Andy had saved her a seat next to him again. She pushed down the fear in her stomach.

'It's going to be the high point of the week in more ways than one,' Andy commented as they settled down. 'The sheerest rock face. Then. Bingo. Over and down!'

'It doesn't seem real,' Zoe said. 'Are we really going to try and abseil down a sheer rock face, Andy?' She felt her nerve going. 'It suddenly feels like the daftest thing in the world to do.'

'We'll be all right, Zoe. We'll do it,' Andy said.

Zoe liked the 'we'. It sounded – nice. Like they were an item.

Mr Wright walked round the bus making encouraging noises.

'Are you going to do it then, Sir?' Andy asked him.

'You bet your life. Wouldn't miss it for the world,' he said. But he had a strange look on his face.

'How about you, Miss?' Meena asked Miss Arnold.

Miss Arnold screwed up her nose. 'It might,' she said, 'and then again, it might not, surprise you to know that the thought terrifies me, Meena. But all for one and one for all. I shall give it my best.'

'And me, Miss,' someone boasted.

'And me.'

'And me.'

'What about you, Miss?' someone asked Miss Grear.

Who looked unfazed. 'Nothing to it,' she said with a shrug of the shoulder.

Frankie shrugged too. But brilliant eyes in a pale strained face gave her away.

The first part of the day was spent exploring the area. 'This'll get the circulation going. Get the nerves under control,' Gary said, striding off and drawing them after him.

'Who said anything about nerves?' Kevin shouted after him.

The scenery was spectacular. Walls of rock. Pointed crags and huge boulders. At one point, Andy stood, legs spread-eagled on a crag and waved and yelled till the hills echoed round him.

Zoe waved and yelled back at him.

Then Gary and Pete led them to a hidden waterfall. Only the roar, which got louder as they got nearer to it, gave them a clue where it was. And when they finally saw it, it was awesome. Gary and Pete knew a way through it. And as they led them through, Zoe felt so excited she couldn't speak.

For the next few hours, Gary and Pete gently encouraged and persuaded even the most reluctant of them – even Frankie – to do a little more.

Then.

The moment of truth!

Unknowingly, Gary and Pete had led them up a slope that ended in a sheer drop...

...They took turns to look over the edge.

'Wicked.'

'Cool.'

'Crazy.'

One or two wouldn't even look. One or two turned pale.

While ropes etc. were being prepared, Gary sat them down on the grass. 'Take your time and think about it,' he said. 'There's no rush.' He studied solemn faces. 'But I do think that anyone who doesn't at least have a try, will regret it later.'

'Not likely. No chance!' Frankie said, slumped down at a safe distance from the edge.

'You're such a wet blanket this week, Frankie,' Kevin Kingdom called. 'Where's your sense of adventure, eh?'

Frankie leapt up. Hurled herself at Kevin and thumped him on the back.

Kevin, taken by surprise, went flying, tottering dangerously near the edge.

Mr Wright grabbed him.

Gary glared at Frankie. 'That was very, very stupid,'

he said, white-faced. 'This isn't the place for petty rivalry. And you're not the only one who's nervous, Frankie.' He looked at everybody. 'Nobody's going to be forced to do anything they don't want to,' he said quietly.

Frankie turned her back on everybody.

Odd one out! Zoe was *so* glad it wasn't her. She even felt a bit sorry for Frankie.

Then Miss Grear got up and strode to the edge.

'I'll go first,' she said briskly.

Today, she'd abandoned her familiar make-up and looked fresh faced. Tendrils of hair escaped from her safety helmet. And she was wearing cheerful red leggings tucked into red and black striped socks, and a red fleece. She didn't look a bit like the person she usually was, and as she disappeared over the edge – just like that! – making it seem like it was the easiest thing in the world to do. Zoe decided they didn't know Miss Grear at all. Someone else they'd misjudged.

There was a communal gasp as she disappeared. Then everyone leaned over and stretched their necks. They held their breath as she bobbed and kicked deftly against rock on the way down.

'Dig that,' Andy said. 'Who'd have thought it of her, eh?'

It was more than a surprise. Everyone was impressed and Miss Grear's reputation was raised in a flash. There was a roar of approval when she reached the bottom.

She looked up with a broad grin on her face and saluted them.

'That's a good start,' Gary said, approvingly. 'Seeing someone go down like that's a terrific help.' He turned aside to Mr Wright and Miss Arnold. 'The level of support and sense of teamwork at a time like this is crucial. It's all a matter of motivation. So?' He looked steadily at Mr Wright, then Miss Arnold. 'Any volunteers for who goes next?'

Mr Wright strutted to the edge. Stopped. Peered over. Then turned back. He suddenly looked as green as the grass he slumped down on.

'Sorry. I've never had a very good head for heights,' he admitted, apologetically.

'It's all right,' Gary said. 'It's important that everyone recognises and accepts their own personal strengths and limitations. It's fine.' He leaned over and patted Mr Wright on the back as if he was comforting one of the kids.

Gary went up even farther in Zoe's estimation.

Miss Arnold walked to the edge and looked over.

'Go on, Arny!' Andy shouted.

Miss Arnold hesitated. But not for long. Next thing she was strapped up and ready to go. And as she went over the edge they cheered wildly.

When she landed she saluted, too.

Gary waited for everyone to calm down, then raised his eyebrows and lowered his chin. 'So. Who's next, then?'

Andy nodded his head sideways at Zoe. 'What about her? What about it, Zo? You can do it!'

Zoe gulped. She couldn't believe Andy had that sort of confidence in her. But it did the trick. She got up and they slapped palms. Then she walked to the edge.

'I'm next, after you,' Andy said, encouraging her.

Mr Wright got up. He was looking better. He and Gary both helped to strap her up.

Miss Grear and Miss Arnold were encouraging her at the bottom...

Her feet swivelled on the edge of nothingness.

Her heart lurched. Her head swam. A picture of Tod came into her head and she wished he could see her now. He'd never accuse her of being boring again.

'Take it easy. Compose yourself,' Gary was saying. 'Plant your feet firm.'

'Feet firm!' she said in a squeaky voice.

Feet planted. Body hanging. Suspended over the sheerest drop she'd ever seen.

'Don't look down,' Miss Grear called from below.

'Keep your feet where they are till they're horizontal. Then ease yourself over,' Gary said quietly. 'There you go, gently does it,' he encouraged her, as she inched her feet over the edge.

'That's the worst bit over,' he said. 'Now. Down! See you in a bit, at the bottom.'

It was heart-stopping.

Weird.

And wonderful...

She fell into Miss Grear's waiting arms. 'Well done, Zoe,' she said.

Then Zoe stared upwards and saluted.

Everyone saluted her back.

Zoe was so proud she could burst. 'It's easy. Honestly!' she yelled up to Andy, who was getting ready to come down now.

And when he was down, Mr Wright had another try. And this time he was fine. Later, he told Zoe it was seeing her had done it.

Then after him, most of the others.

One or two didn't attempt it though. They were content just to peep over the edge.

But Frankie totally lost it. She was almost hysterical.

'It's all right, Frankie,' Gary insisted. 'I'll say it again. It's important for everyone to recognise and accept their personal strengths and limitations. It's fine not to do this.'

But Frankie hated being the one sitting forlornly looking down.

'It's not all right,' she said through closed teeth.

For the rest of the day, she had the same closed expression on her face. While Zoe felt as if she was walking on air...

And after dinner that night, Zoe was one of the few who ventured out to do the shortened, floodlit, version of the assault course. It was an 'extra' – for those who wanted to do it.

Andy did it too.

Sliding down zip wires in the glare of the floodlights, the background a black inky darkness, was wonderful. Under and over and through the nets with Andy.

The whole day had been like a dream.

Chapter Fourteen

On the last complete day of activities, the mood of everybody was more relaxed. The main event of the day was orienteering. Which sounded easy after yesterday. And to round off things that night, there were notices around the place advertising Revels Round the Campfire, which would, according to Pete, be the social highlight of the week.

Gary checked their footwear and clothing. Then gave out maps and description sheets.

Pete gave them the pep talk.

'The aim? Find your way to an unknown destination. Teams will leave at timed intervals. The team who gets to the destination in the shortest time, wins.'

Andy and Zoe were in the same team, with Faye Cooper and Miss Grear. Matt Baker and Kevin Kingdom made up the rest of the team.

'Look well if we get lost, Andy,' Zoe said.

'Get lost? No way, Zo. We've got maps. And we can read them. That's what they're for, you know,' he teased her.

Zoe didn't mind Andy teasing her.

They'd practised map reading at school, but Pete warned them that the real thing could turn out to be more difficult.

'If you try to take short cuts and don't stick to the map, it will be a case of more haste and less speed,' he advised. 'So use the map. Then you will know exactly where you're going—'

'—and then you can enjoy yourselves,' Gary added.

'And that's the most important thing of all,' Pete said.

'Orienteering around here—' Gary said, then paused as if he was searching for words. '—it's the best thing ever.' His eyes shone. 'Fantastic countryside and fabulous woodland to go through. And peace and quiet to enjoy it. Remember to look and listen for the wildlife too.'

His enthusiasm was infectious. Except in certain quarters.

'Blow the peace and quiet. I'd give anything to be surrounded by traffic and shops and people,' Frankie muttered.

'Look out for the markers,' Pete reminded them. 'And when you get to the control points, use your description sheets. Then double check. And it'll be a cinch.'

Zoe's group started at a run. Did exactly what they were told and followed the map. Bursting with energy and determination and enthusiasm, it led them straight to the first control point.

Miss Grear held up the description sheet: '"You will see a yellow flag on top of a rock, the river on your left, a peak on your right." she read.

Each of them checked the description and double checked.

There it was. The peak. The river. The flag.

'Easy peasy, Miss!' Zoe said.

Miss Grear nodded.

Then it was back to the map and on to the next point.

'"You will see a yellow flag in a hollow tree just off the path to your left. There's a fallen tree to your right, a bridle path forks to your right. Take the bridle path next." ' Zoe read. The fallen tree was there. But where was the hollow tree? 'There!' Zoe yelled.

Check the description. Double check.

Back to the map and onto the next point.

"A yellow flag at the entrance to a cave on your left." Search. Check. Double check...

It was during stops to get their breath and bearings that they could appreciate what Gary had said. Marvelling at the trees that soared endlessly up into the sky, their tops reaching heights that made them dizzy. At the sun breaking through the canopy, making a kaleidoscope effect of shadow and light. At the mesmerising sound of the water as it flowed and gushed and gurgled over stones in the river bed. At the sounds and sights of the birds and insects as they flashed through the trees. Everyone, like Gary, was awe-struck by it.

'Two more control points and we're home!' Kevin said after one of these stops. And they upped the pace...

Breathless, exhilarated, and totally up yours! they arrived at the destination and booked in.

So far they were the fastest team. Though they'd have to wait for the others to finish before it could all be worked out properly.

Gary shook their hands and gave each of them a certificate of completion.

Teams trickled in, red-faced, huffing and puffing, and exhilarated. And Gary congratulated everyone of them. Everyone of them was awarded a certificate of completion.

Except Frankie's team. Which still hadn't arrived, long past the time they should have.

In the same team as Frankie were Amy and Meena. Anita Patel and Natalie Yates. And Miss Arnold.

Everyone waited impatiently. But as more time passed and there was still no sign of them, mutters of irritation turned to murmurs of concern.

And when even more time passed and there was still no sign of them, Gary began to look decidedly worried.

Another ten minutes and he alerted Pete on his radio control. It wasn't possible to get clear enough signals in the area to use mobile phones.

Within the time it took Pete to join them, everything had changed. Everyone was now very worried. And finally, an emergency was declared.

All adult personnel available from the Centre were called out for a search of the area. Leaving a skeleton staff to supervise the rest of them, who were sent back to the Centre.

Once back there, all they could do was wait. And mope. Bitterly disappointed. Things were supposed to have finished on a brilliant climax round the camp fire. But instead, they were grinding to a slow, drawn out and uncertain end.

Kids huddled together in tense clusters as the day drew to a close. It had been warm and dry all day, but now it began to rain. Everybody's imagination was now working overtime.

For the first time since leaving school on Monday morning, the minutes dragged. And no one knew how to fill them.

Angie, the cook, said things like this didn't happen here. 'We've got a marvellous record for safety,' she said. Then she began to mutter words like hypothermia under her breath.

Finally, a rescue team arrived to help in the search. Everyone strained to hear what was being said.

'We'll let you know as soon as there's any news,' Gary promised them before setting out again with the rescue team.

But they all wanted to get out there and search too.

'Can't we help, Gary?' several kids begged.

'You're not familiar with the countryside. It would be foolish to let any of you go anywhere now,' Gary said. 'But thanks.'

Zoe was gutted. For once in her life things had been going right and she'd been revelling in it. Now it was spoiled. But then, when she thought about Frankie and the others and their parents, and Miss Arnold, she felt ashamed of herself.

'Frankie didn't really want to come in the first place, did she?' she said to Andy.

After a very long and very uncomfortable wait that seemed to go on for ever, there was suddenly a shout that the group had been found and were on their way into the Centre with the rescue team right now.

There was an audible gasp, then everybody stampeded to the entrance hall.

Where they saw a cold, wet, and bedraggled group. But no Frankie!

Chapter Fifteen

There was a shocked silence.

'Where's Frankie?' someone shouted.

'Frankie had an accident,' Pete said, as if things weren't that straightforward. 'She's all right. But they took her to hospital to make sure she's not suffering from concussion. And they're keeping her in overnight for observation.'

There was a communal sigh of relief.

The rest of the team looked tired, cold and exhausted.

Meena smiled shakily. 'It's great to be back. We're OK now,' she said. But she could hardly stand.

Zoe ran up to her and put an arm round her.

'Everyone's OK. No real damage done, fortunately...' one of the search party said. But he too spoke as if it wasn't that straightforward.

Mr Wright and Miss Grear checked that everyone was in fact all right. Then the cook, Angie, bustled up. 'Let's get them in the bath, and warmed up,' she said and put an arm round Amy.

Pete said for everyone else to go into the lounge, where he wanted to talk to them.

They were all ears.

'You may as well hear the official version from me,' he said. 'Frankie James thought she'd skip the orienteering and go off on a jaunt with Amy Enright. They gave the team the slip. Found the road. Intending to hitch a lift to the nearest town. But they didn't get a lift, and the road petered out, as they do in this area. Then they were lost.' His mouth was now tight and angry. 'It was a stupid thing to do. The road became a dust track to nowhere. Then it began to rain. They found a barn. It was then Frankie had her accident.' The hint of a smile appeared on his face. 'They were trying to get into the barn to shelter, when a piece of the barn door collapsed and hit Frankie on the head. Thankfully, the farmer heard the noise and went to investigate.' He laughed wryly. 'Frankie's version of him turning up, complete with shotgun, will no doubt become the stuff of legend at your school!' He sighed. 'Anyway. The farmer called us then.' He paused. 'In the meantime, the rest of the team had got lost because they went off course looking for the two of them. And they're the ones I feel sorry for.'

Gary put his head round the door. 'It's stopped raining, Pete. And all the preparations were done hours ago. What do you think?'

Pete looked at the kids. 'Is anyone still up to the campfire revels?'

There was a huge cheer.

Memories of Zoe's last big social event flooded back.

The Christmas Disco. Ending up in the empty classroom.

She shuddered. But then hugged herself. Tonight things were going to be different, she was quite sure...

Its lateness made the event even more special. And when Miss Arnold appeared with the others, there was a loud cheer. Amy was very subdued. The only one missing now, was Frankie.

Gary and Miss Grear brought out guitars – Miss Grear had been full of surprises on this trip – and they played together.

Pete led the singing round the huge fire. Scout songs. Pop songs. Silly songs. Sad songs. Happy songs. Sloppy songs.

No one had thought about food for hours and suddenly everyone was starving. They ate ravenously. Frizzled sausages, burgers, kebabs and fish. Field mushrooms and baked beans. Potatoes in their jackets.

Everyone was on a high as the firelight cast its shadows, and beyond the shadows darkness enclosed them.

Andy tugged Zoe's sleeve and pointed to where some kids had got up to dance.

Shyly, she got up to dance with him.

It was magic...

That night in bed, Zoe thought about going home. Telling Mel about Andy. Wouldn't she be surprised? And wouldn't Tod be envious when she told him about everything she'd done?

Then there was school. She'd got to know classmates so much better this week. And it would never go back to what it was like before.

Then there was Andy...

Frankie arrived back at the Centre in the morning, apparently none the worse for her experience. They were on their way home and that's all she seemed interested in.

When they boarded the bus, she plonked herself down on the back seat and gathered her buddies to her. 'Thank God we're on our way back to civilisation,' she said loudly and belligerently.

But no one responded. Not even her buddies.

Everyone else was sorry to be leaving.

This time Zoe had no worries about where to sit or who with. Andy had waited for her and got on the bus with her.

They settled down.

Frankie will never get to me again, Zara, Zoe said, staring out of the window.

'What did you say?' Andy said.

Zoe hadn't realised she'd spoken aloud. 'Oh. It's nothing, Andy,' she said. 'Just kids' stuff.'

She offered no further explanation. Zara had been there for her when she needed her. Always would be, she supposed. Only now, somehow, she didn't seem important.

'It's good to have real friends, isn't it, Andy?' she said.

'Sure,' Andy said. 'Anything you say, Zo.'

Zoe frowned thoughtfully. 'One day though,' she said softly, 'when I have a little girl, I'm going to call her Zara.'

Andy laughed. 'OK. Fine by me. But we're not even engaged yet are we, Zo?'

Zoe hit him. 'Don't be daft,' she said.

But I mean it, Zara, she said. *That's a promise.*